So Many Feelings
Sign Language for Feelings and Emotions

by Dawn Babb Prochovnic
illustrated by Stephanie Bauer

Content Consultant:
Lora Heller, MS, MT-BC, LCAT
and Founding Director of Baby Fingers LLC

magic wagon

visit us at www.abdopublishing.com

For Carli and Justin. I feel happy when I'm around you—DP
For Sophie and Johanna, the bestest of friends!—SB

Published by Magic Wagon, a division of the ABDO Group, PO Box 398166, Minneapolis, Minnesota 55439.

Printed in the United States of America, North Mankato, Minnesota.
102011
012012
This book contains at least 10% recycled materials.

Written by Dawn Babb Prochovnic
Illustrations by Stephanie Bauer
Edited by Stephanie Hedlund and Rochelle Baltzer
Cover and interior layout and design by Neil Klinepier

Story Time with Signs & Rhymes provides an introduction to ASL vocabulary through stories that are written and structured in English. ASL is a separate language with its own structure. Just as there are personal and regional variations in spoken and written languages, there are similar variations in sign language.

Library of Congress Cataloging-in-Publication Data

Prochovnic, Dawn Babb.
  So many feelings : sign language for feelings and emotions / by Dawn Babb Prochovnic ; illustrated by Stephanie Bauer.
      p. cm. -- (Story time with signs & rhymes)
  Summary: Playful stories in simple rhymes introduce the American Sign Language signs for feelings and emotions.
  ISBN 978-1-61641-841-0
  1. American Sign Language--Juvenile fiction. 2. Stories in rhyme. 3. Emotions--Juvenile fiction. [1. Emotions--Fiction. 2. Sign language. 3. Stories in rhyme.] I. Bauer, Stephanie, ill. II. Title. III. Series: Story time with signs & rhymes.
  PZ10.4.P76So 2012
  [E]--dc23
                        2011027076

Alphabet Handshapes

American Sign Language (ASL) is a visual language that uses handshapes, movements, and facial expressions. Sometimes people spell English words by making the handshape for each letter in the word they want to sign. This is called fingerspelling. The pictures below show the handshapes for each letter in the manual alphabet.

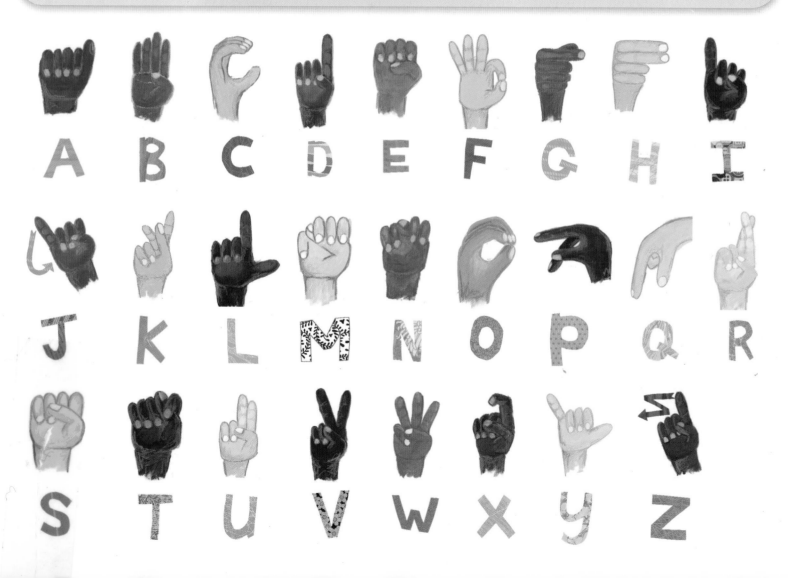

José feels **excited**.
He scored a home run.
"I love playing baseball!
Yahoo! Our team won!"

excited

Belinda is **happy**.
She giggles and squeals.
"I'm learning to balance
without training wheels!"

happy

"I'm **proud**," says Hiroshi.
"I worked really hard.
I planted a garden
in Papa's backyard."

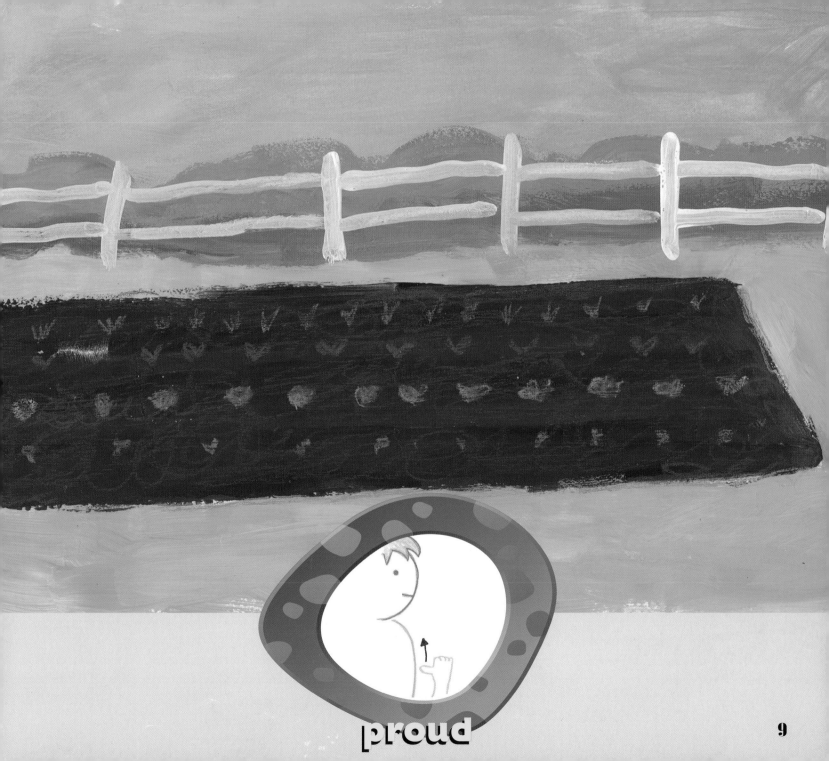

proud

Melissa is **grumpy**.
She grabs her stuffed bear,
then shouts at her brother,
"I don't want to share!"

grumpy

Dakota feels guilty
but still tells a lie:
"I just saw our dog eat
the last piece of pie."

guilty

"I'm **sad**," cries Naomi,
"I lost the big race.
I practiced all season
but finished last place."

FINISH

sad

15

Patricia is **lonely**.
Her friend moved away.
"I hope that Sabrina
can visit someday."

lonely

"I'm **scared**," whispers Henry.
"I don't like this place.
That monster looks spooky
with blood on his face."

scared

Rebecca feels **nervous**.
Her heart beats *thump-thump*.
"I hope I don't fall when
it's my turn to jump."

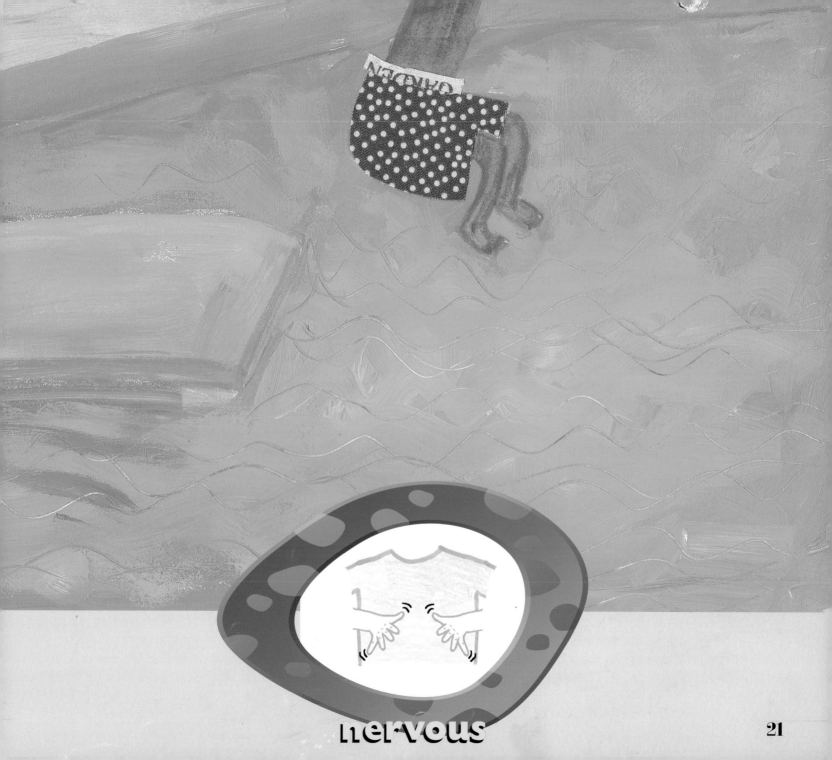

nervous

"I'm **mad!**" hollers Betsy.
"Kate messed up my game.
She stole all the marbles,
then called me a name."

mad

Lorenzo is sorry
for hurting Marie.
"Here is a bandage
to put on your knee."

24

sorry

Renee is **embarrassed.**
Her face is bright red.
She burped at the wedding.
"Excuse me," she said.

26

embarrassed

American Sign Language Glossary

embarrassed: Hold your hands in front of your face with your palms facing in and your fingertips pointing up. Now move your hands in alternating arcs, up and away from your face. Repeat this a couple of times. It should look like you are showing blood rising into your cheeks because you are embarrassed.

excited: Touch your chest with the middle finger of your "Five Hands" as you move your hands in alternating circles, up and out from your chest. Your palms should be facing in, and your face should look excited.

grumpy: With a grumpy look on your face, hold your curved "Five Hand" in front of your face near your mouth. Your palm should be facing toward you. Now straighten and curve your fingers a couple of times. It should look like you are showing the tension you are feeling.

guilty: Tap your "G Hand" near your chest just above your heart, with your palm facing left.

happy: With a smile on your face, brush your chest with the palm of your hand a couple of times. Your hand should be moving up and out from your chest. If you are especially happy you might use two hands for this sign, and you would put a bigger smile on your face.

lonely: Hold your pointer finger near your lips. Now move your hand in a small circle toward your chin and back to your lips.

mad: Hold your curved "Five Hand" in front of your chest. Your palm should be facing toward you and your eyes and forehead should be scrunched so you look angry. Now move your hand toward your face in one sharp motion as you clench your fingers a little tighter. It should look like you are showing the tension you are feeling and should look more intense than the sign for grumpy.

nervous: Bend your elbows. Hold your hands near the sides of your body and quickly shake them a few times. It should look like you are shaky because you are nervous.

proud: Touch the thumb of your "A Hand" to the middle of your chest, then move your hand up toward the top of your chest. Your palm should be facing down, and your chest should look strong and boastful as if it is bursting with pride.

sad: Hold your hands in front of your face with your palms facing toward you and your fingertips pointing up. Now pull your hands down toward your chin as you droop your eyes and make a long, sad face. It should look like you are showing the tears coming from your eyes.

scared: Bend your elbows. Make two fists and hold them close to the sides of your body with your palms facing your chest. Now, quickly move your hands closer together and open your hands. Your fingers should be spread out and your face should look scared as if you have just been startled.

sorry: Make a fist and rub small circles on your chest near your heart. Your palm should be facing in. Your face should look like you are feeling sorry and regretful.

Fun Facts about ASL

Most sign language dictionaries describe how a sign looks for a right-handed signer. If you are left-handed, you would modify the instructions so the signs feel more comfortable to you. For example, to sign *guilty*, a left-handed signer would tap the left "G Hand" on the chest, with the palm facing right.

Facial expressions and body language are an important part of communicating in sign language, and they are especially important when communicating emotions. To communicate fully and clearly, your facial expressions and body language should match the emotion you are signing. For example, when you sign *sad*, you should have a sad look on your face, and you should slouch your body and droop your head. When you sign *proud*, your face should look pleased, and you should stand tall with your chest out.

A sign can communicate different degrees of emotion based on how it is made. For example, to communicate that you are *very sorry*, you would exaggerate the sign for sorry by rubbing your chest more dramatically than usual while slumping your shoulders and showing a more regretful expression on your face.

Signing Activities

Guess My Emotion: This is a fun activity for partners. Take turns being the actor. The first actor uses body language and facial expressions to communicate one of the emotions listed in the glossary. The partner makes the sign for the emotion being shown. When the partner makes the correct sign, switch roles. Continue taking turns until you and your partner have correctly made the signs for each emotion mentioned in the book.

Make a Feelings Poster: Get a piece of construction paper, some blank index cards, and tape. On the top of the construction paper write, "Today I Feel." Now take one index card and position it horizontally in the middle of the construction paper. Use this index card to create a "pocket" by taping the bottom and sides of the index card to the construction paper. Near the top of each of the remaining index cards, write the word for one emotion from the glossary. Now, think about how you are feeling today and select a card to match that feeling. Slide the card into the pocket you created. If you want others to know how you are feeling, tuck the card into the pocket only part of the way so the feeling word can be seen. If you want your feelings to be private, tuck the card into the pocket so the feeling word cannot be seen.

Additional Resources

Further Reading

Coleman, Rachel. *Once Upon a Time* (Signing Time DVD, Series 2, Volume 11). Two Little Hands Productions, 2008.

Edge, Nellie. *ABC Phonics: Sing, Sign, and Read!* Northlight Communications, 2010.

Heller, Lora. *Sign Language for Kids*. Sterling, 2004.

Valli, Clayton. *The Gallaudet Dictionary of American Sign Language*. Gallaudet University Press, 2005.

Web Sites

To learn more about ASL, visit ABDO Group online at **www.abdopublishing.com**. Web sites about ASL are featured on our Book Links page. These links are routinely monitored and updated to provide the most current information available.